Narrator, King Stefan, and King Hubert   Bob Holt
Maleficent and Merryweather   Linda Gray

Once Upon a Dream (02:47)
Performed by Mary Costa, Bill Shirley, and Chorus
Music and Lyrics by Sammy Fain and Jack Lawrence
© 1952 Walt Disney Music Company (ASCAP). © renewed.
All rights reserved. International © renewed.
℗ 1959 Walt Disney Records

℗ 2008 Walt Disney Records
© Disney

This edition published by Parragon in 2010
Parragon
Queen Street House
4 Queen Street
Bath BA1 1HE, UK

ISBN 978-1-4454-2402-6

Manufactured in China

Sleeping Beauty

Bath · New York · Singapore · Hong Kong · Cologne · Delhi
Melbourne · Amsterdam · Johannesburg · Auckland · Shenzhen

In a far away land, long ago, lived King Stefan and his fair Queen. One day a daughter was born and they called her Aurora. They named her after the dawn, for she filled their lives with sunshine.

From near and far the people came, bringing their gifts, to celebrate the royal birth.

The most honoured guests were the three good fairies: Fauna, Flora and Merryweather. Each could give the child a single gift. Flora blessed the child with beauty. Fauna gave the gift of song, that she might sing like a nightingale.

Little Merryweather was about to give her gift when suddenly there was a roar of thunder and a gust of wind. A blinding flash of light filled the great hall, and before them stood the evil Maleficent. "Well, King Stefan. I was quite upset at not receiving an invitation. I, too, have a gift to bestow on the child."

"The princess shall indeed grow in grace and beauty. But before the sun sets on her sixteenth birthday, she shall prick her finger on the spindle of a spinning wheel, and die!"

"Oh, no!" The cry rose from every heart. But before anyone could seize Maleficent and make her take back her evil curse, she had vanished in a flash of flame. What a terrible situation! But there was hope. Merryweather still had her gift to give. "Your Majesties, I cannot undo this wicked curse, but I can help."

Merryweather waved her magic wand over the cradle.

"Sweet Princess, if all this should come to pass, not in death, but just in sleep, the fateful prophecy you will keep. And from this slumber you shall awake, when True Love's Kiss the spell shall break."

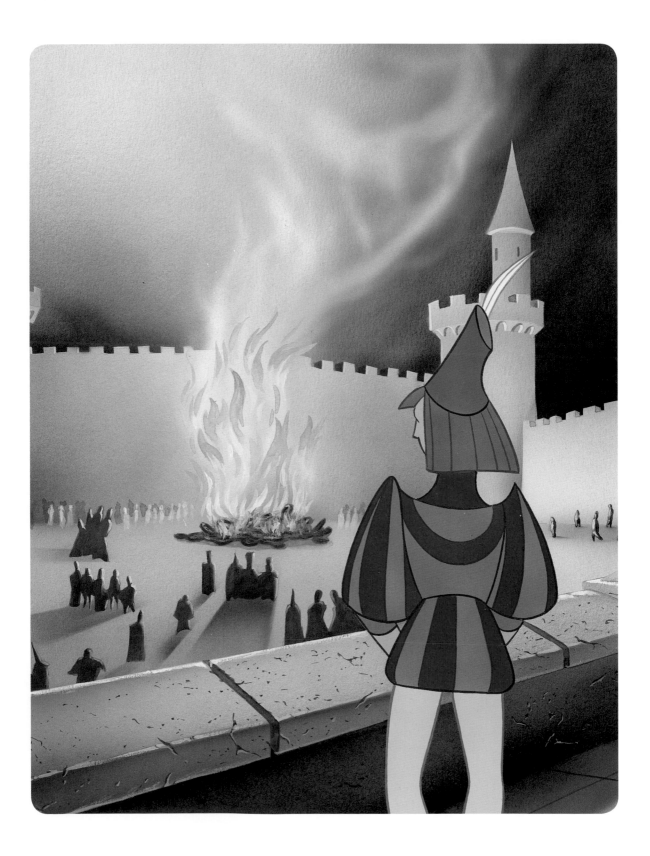

But King Stefan was still fearful for his daughter's life.

"This does not take away the evil threat. We must take action! Let every spindle and spinning wheel in the country be burned!"

That night, the countryside was aglow with the light of burning spinning wheels.

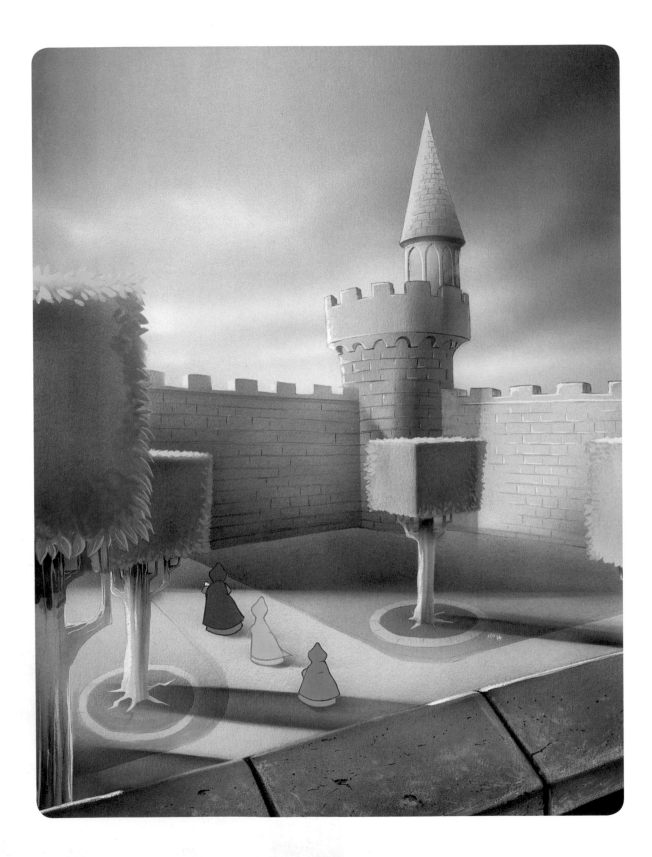

Meanwhile, the three good fairies were trying to think of a better plan. Merryweather told the others, "A bonfire won't stop Maleficent. There must be some way we can protect Aurora from that wicked old witch! I know, let us raise the Princess in a secret hiding place. We will keep her safe until her sixteenth birthday." Sadly, the King and Queen agreed.

Disguised as simple peasant women, the three good fairies took the young Princess to a tiny cottage deep in the woods. They called her Briar Rose instead of Aurora, and never told her she was a Princess. So for sixteen years, the whereabouts of Aurora remained a mystery.

On her sixteenth birthday, Briar Rose was picking berries, when she chanced to meet a handsome young man riding in the forest. He was very kind. She was rather shy.

She was not supposed to speak with strangers, but Briar Rose felt as if she knew him, for she had often dreamed of meeting someone so charming.

She asked him to come to the cottage that evening and meet her family. Then Briar Rose rushed home to tell Flora, Fauna and Merryweather her happy news.

She was falling in love.

When Briar Rose told the fairy godmothers about her true love, they grew sad. "Since it's your sixteenth birthday, we must tell you the truth now. You are really the Princess Aurora. Your marriage to Prince Phillip will take place this very evening in your father's castle. You can never see your handsome stranger again." Briar Rose burst into tears.

Meanwhile, the young stranger rode off to tell his father that he had just met the girl of his dreams. Actually, the young man was Prince Phillip. When he told his father, King Hubert, about Briar Rose, the King became very upset.

🌹 ♡ 🌷

"What? You've fallen in love with some peasant girl?
I won't have it! I promised my neighbour, King Stefan, that
you would marry his daughter Aurora! You're a Prince! And
you're going to marry a Princess!"

But Phillip's mind was made up. Off he rode to the
cottage in the woods to meet his true love, Briar Rose.

But she was not there. The three good fairies had carefully escorted her to King Stefan's castle. The poor Princess should have been happy, but all she could think of was her lost love.

Merryweather led her up to her room.

"Cheer up, dear. You can't meet your father looking so glum. We'll leave you alone for a few moments to dry your tears."

"Listen! It's Maleficent!" The fairies rushed through the palace corridors searching for the Princess. "Rose! Rose! Don't touch anything!"

But Maleficent's curse was far too powerful. The evil fairy called out from the shadows. "Touch the spindle. Touch it, I say!" As if in a dream, Aurora stretched out her hand to touch the shining spindle.

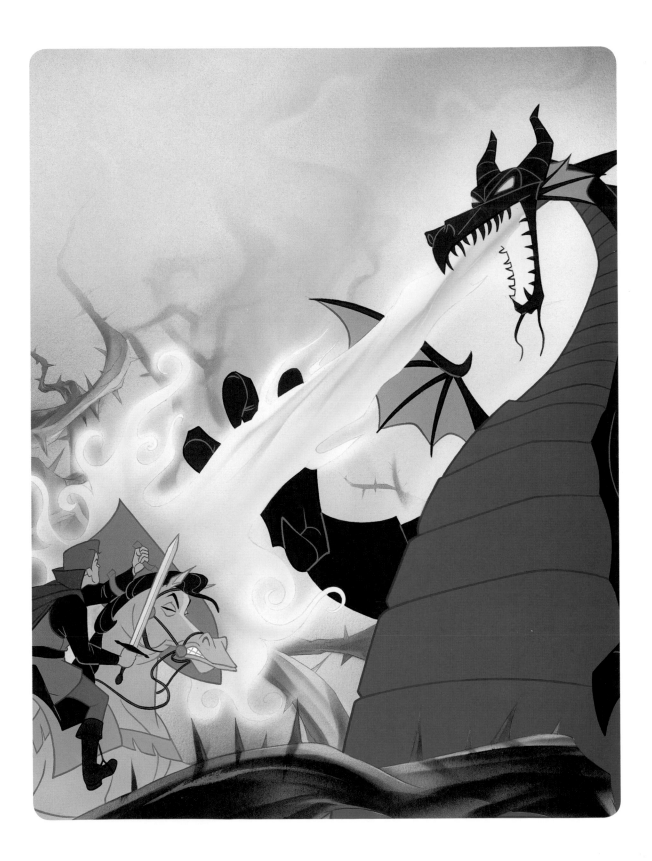

Maleficent was furious when she found that the Prince had escaped. Determined to stop him, she turned herself into a fiery dragon. But her evil could not overcome Phillip's magic sword and his true love. Maleficent was destroyed.

With the help of the three fairies, Prince Phillip found the tiny tower room where his sleeping beauty lay.

There, dreaming of her true love, was the Princess Aurora – the very same girl he had fallen in love with.

He gave her a kiss. She opened her eyes and smiled. Maleficent's spell was broken.

Soon the whole castle was awake and the joyous wedding celebration began.

And so the Sleeping Beauty and her own true love were married and lived happily ever after.

Now you have finished reading the story of
Sleeping Beauty, why not sing along
with this fun song from the movie?

ONCE UPON A DREAM

Music and Lyrics by Sammy Fain and Jack Lawrence
Performed by Mary Costa, Bill Shirley and Chorus

I know you, I walked with you once upon a dream

I know you, the gleam in your eyes is

so familiar a gleam

Yet I know it's true that visions are seldom

all they seem

But if I know you I know what you'll do

You'll love me at once the way you did once

Upon a dream

La, la, la...

But if I know you I know what you'll do
You'll love me at once the way you did once
Upon a dream
I know you, I walked with you once
upon a dream
I know you, the gleam in your eyes
is so familiar a gleam
And I know it's true that visions are
seldom all they seem
But if I know you I know what you'll do
You'll love me at once the way you did once
Upon a dream.